Hope and Hilarity

Positive Stories of
Faith, Family, and Fun.

**Written by
Chuck Terrill**

**Illustrated by
Bryan Clark**

Copyright © 1996

Chuck Terrill
All Rights Reserved

Library of Congress Catalog Card Number:
96-90484

ISBN: 1-57502-266-4

Morris Publishing
Kearney, Nebraska

To Mary...
*my wife and my friend,
and to my children,
Chris, Sarah and Ben...*

*All proceeds of this book
benefit the
Haverhill Christian Church
Building Fund.*

In Gratitude......

There are several dear ladies I must thank who have been a creative force in my life. Many thanks belong to my mother Ella Mae and to my Grannies Thelma and Mertie.

My wife Mary deserves my greatest thanks, admiration, and love. Agnes Nibarger has been the best "surrogate" Mom a boy could ask for. I could not do without Sarah, Jeanette, Debra, Lisa Marie, or Ellana Marie, either.

I certainly appreciate Bryan Clark's genius in illustrating these stories. God has given him a great gift which he uses well. Thanks also to Crystal Elliott, Jodi Kenyon, and Marsha Stom for editing this book.

I also owe a great debt to my family and friends who never dreamed they would become the unwitting focus of my stories.

I am also grateful for my friends in the Mulberry and Haverhill Christian Churches. It has been a joy to serve you.

I owe my greatest thanks to Jesus Christ, My Lord and Savior.

TABLE OF CONTENTS

Of Kitchens and Doghouses	7
The Demise of Marriage	10
Kids Say the Darndest Things	13
The Party Line	17
The Preacher's Garden	20
It is a Mystery to Me	23
A Little Glimpse of Heaven	35
Reunions and Unintentional Sin	39
Stuffy Sunday Mornings	42
Light From Grannie's Life	45
Lessons From a Well	48
Musings on a Screen Door	51
Leonard's Pond	55
One of Life's Little Lessons	61
A Memory of the Fourth of July	65
Mother's Derserve a "Thank You."	68

TABLE OF CONTENTS *(Continued)*

In Search of Rest	71
We Got By With Murder	74
Please Pass the Biscuits	77
A Lesson Learned	80
Time to Give Thanks	86
Upended By Foolish Pride	89
Things That Didn't Happen	94
Thanksgiving Cornucopia	98
The Fire is Out	102
Watching the Fire Spread	105
Grandpa's Coffee	108
Nitcher's Grocery Store	110
I heard an Angel's Voice	113
All Thigs Work Together for Good	118
Welcome Home	121
Memories of Christmas Past	124
Looking For Christmas	127
Is There Room for Christ?	132
Got your Wood Laid By?	136
A Great Teacher	138

Of Kitchens and Dog Houses

It looks like I'm in trouble again. I hear Mrs. Preacher in the kitchen clanging and banging her pots and pans around. That's how I know it is serious. While I'm in the doghouse, she bakes.

Married folks settle their spats in a variety of ways. Normal ways. We lived next door to a couple who could argue well past midnight. Others use the silent treatment. Some women are exceptional criers, while their husbands major in pouting. We even knew a couple who would occasionally throw things at each other. Not so with us. My wife bakes. Once, when we were newlyweds, I thought I'd intrude when she was "cookin' mad." I peeked around the corner of the door and changed my mind.

She body slammed a big batch of dough on the counter. She slapped it all around the edges and then punched in its middle. Hard. She picked it up, flipped it, and smashed it on the counter in a way that would make Hulk Hogan envious.

After she beat up the dough real good, she pinched a chunk and twisted it off. It caused me to envision the Pillsbury Dough Boy ® losing his ears.

I retreated quietly to the living room.

> **"But if your enemy is hungry, feed him, and if he is thirsty, give him a drink; for in so doing you will heap burning coals upon his head."**

I hate it when she bakes like that.

I wish she would just get it over with, do something sane like cry, yell, or pout.

But no! She has to come in and thrust a steaming homemade cinnamon roll in my face. What a predicament! To be madder than blue blazes and have a fresh cinnamon roll under your nose!

"I'll show her. I'm tough. I don't have to eat her stinkin' cinnamon roll," I tell myself as I push it aside.

"What's the use," I sigh as I polish off the last of it. "I love the woman. she may not know how to fight, but she sure knows how to cook."

I get up and go to the kitchen to tell her so. We eat another cinnamon roll together and the world is right again.

So if we run into you at the grocery store, and our cart is full of baking stuff, and you think we're putting on a little weight . . . well, as Paul Harvey would say, "Now you know the rest of the story."

"Page Two."

"But if your enemy is hungry, feed him, and if he is thirsty, give him a drink; for in so doing you will heap burning coals upon his head" (Romans 12:20, New American Standard Version).

⌘ ⌘ ⌘

The Demise of Marriage

Call me old fashioned, but I still believe in marriage. No one should start a family without one. But it appears that marriage is becoming a relic of the past.
Divorce has reached such an unprecedented rate that single parent homes may become the norm rather than the exception.

I am amused, though saddened by some social workers' and psychologists' answers to our modern day dilemma: "Well, it's mighty hard for women today to keep their home while maintaining a full time job," they say.

Grandma had it much easier. That's why she was so successful at raising her children and keeping her

> **Grandma had it much easier. That's why she was so successful at raising her children and keeping her marriage intact.**

marriage intact.

She had only the non-essential trivialities of life to contend with. She was afforded the luxury of staying in the home so that she could milk the cows at 5 a.m.. Then she got to churn the butter and bake the bread.

After she had scrubbed the week's washing on a board in a galvanized tub and hung it out to dry, she had the pleasure of hoeing corn before she made supper. Yes, she had it made, just ask her. She loved her life!

The demise of marriage can't be blamed on having two breadwinners in the family, that has always been the case. It must be something more subtle. Something like a selfish trend that requires us, male and female, to put ourselves first. It must be something that demands us to believe that we are the center of our own universe.

Apparently, it is a philosophy that our young people have learned quickly and well. In our age of ready mixed, freeze dried, and instant everythings, who really needs a spouse?

We can mix it, fix it, nuke it and shake and bake it all by ourselves. And if we can't, maybe we can get good old Grandma to do it for us.

Let's just pray that we never run out of Grandmas.

⌘ ⌘ ⌘

Kids Say the Darndest Things

I was trying to get the Sunday School children to sing "Jesus Loves the Little Children." If you've ever attended Sunday School anywhere, you know the words to this old favorite. But what the kids in my class sang wasn't the version I knew as a child. They sang this version, climaxed by riotous laughter:

*"Jesus loves the little children;
All the children of the world,
Red and Yellow, Pink and Green
Strangest Kids I've ever seen,
Jesus loves the little children of the world."*

> **"Let the little children come to me, and do not hinder them, for the kingdom of heaven belongs to such as these."**

No, I wasn't offended. It was a serendipity. Whether they knew it or not, they had sung about Christ's willingness to love the unlovely, to accept those who are, by other standards, unacceptable. In their innocent, fun-loving way, those kids had revealed a great truth about God.

Maybe that is why Christ delighted

in letting little children come to Him.

He would listen to them, and surely laugh at their innocent banter. Christ would place His hands upon their heads and pray for them.

Jesus Delights in Spending Time with Children.

How refreshing it must have been for Christ, as He faced the deceit of the religious rulers of His day, to spend time with innocent children. At least they would tell Him the truth, to the best of their ability.

Anyone who has ever taught Youth Sunday School has experienced the forthrightness of their pupils. Children's comments are precious.

According to the students, Noah's wife's name was Joan. "Joan of Ark." I'll bet you didn't know that.

Did you know that the fifth commandment is "Humor thy Father and Mother?"

Have you heard that Lot's wife was "a pillar of salt by day and a ball of fire at night?" You can learn a lot by teaching Sunday School.

Jesus, on His way to the cross, despite the protests of His Disciples, stopped to spend time with children. Listen again to what He said:

"Let the little children come to me, and do not hinder them, for the kingdom of heaven belongs to such as these" (Matthew 19:14, New International Version).

Jesus still delights in spending time with children. Let your children spend time with Him. It's easy. Just take them to Sunday School.

⌘ ⌘ ⌘

The Party Line

We have little difficulty knowing what is going on in the world these days. The television, radio, and newspaper keep us up to date on the latest events. But, for the most part, the news we get is about people we don't know and places we've never been. Do you know what I miss? The party-line.

We used to be on an eight-party party-line, and what was interesting was that we knew all the people on our party line. They lived in our neighborhood. Every household had its own "ring." Our's was "two shorts." We could tell exactly who was getting a call.

And we listened. And because we listened we assumed that others listened to *our* calls as well. It was a simple thing to be careful to say nothing that we didn't want the world to hear! But there was rarely any news that we didn't care to share.

It was a good way to give and get the news. We weren't malicious in our eavesdropping, we were genuinely interested. We knew who was ill, or was coming to visit, or what neighborhood girl was going on her first date, and with whom.

Maybe you miss those days, too. Now we live in an age of FAX machines and can receive the latest news from Timbuctoo in just a few seconds time, but we rarely know our neighbor.

We can cram ourselves into apartment complexes and live for years and never meet the people who live at the end of the hall. Wouldn't it be refreshing to know who is full of special joy over an unexpected event? Do we know who hurts? Do we know who might need our help? Do we even care to know?

I do appreciate the progress that has been made in our lifetime. But I'd still like to hear the phone ring "two shorts" and know that everybody on our party-line knew the call was for me.

Something went out of our lives when we lost the party-line. I hope it wasn't the ability to care for our neighbors.

"Suppose a woman has ten silver coins, but she loses one of them. She will light a lamp and clean house. She will look carefully for the coin until she finds it. When she has found it she will call her friends and neighbors and say, 'Be happy with me! I have found the coin that I lost'" (Luke 15:8-9).

⌘ ⌘ ⌘

The Preacher's Garden

The first thing my garden raised was a few eyebrows. I planted it right next door to the church. In plain sight. It is a little unusual to see a garden planted in a place like that. And people are both amused and amazed to see a hoe wielding, suit wearing pastor tending his garden. But that's okay.

A preacher's garden has to do with

soil preparation. Jesus talked about it in his parable of the sower (Mark 4). There comes a time when all the conditions are right for planting. But first, the preacher has to get down in the row where the delicate infant plants will live. He knows that good gardeners don't just read about gardening. They don't stay in plush offices imagining what it is like to raise a crop. They're in the dirt, breathing, touching, and digging in the plant's real world.

And the preacher's garden has much to do with nurturing and growth. He doesn't know where the tiny plant came

> *"And let us not lose heart in doing good, for in due time we shall reap a harvest if we do not grow weary."*

from, he certainly didn't do it! He simply planted a seed. God did the rest, resulting in new birth.

Now the preacher has the privilege of caring for the new life, the opportunity to measure the progress.

It is a high calling to nurture an

immature plant. Grasshoppers plague it. Aphids infest it. Weeds spring up to choke it and the sun threatens to burn it up. In the garden the preacher has to deal with sin and frustration.

There are weeds to chop with a vengeance. The preacher can work up a sweat in his suit. Even so, he sometimes loses a few plants. He is disappointed, but he trusts in the Lord's promises.

There will be a harvest! The Kingdom will grow! Sometimes imperceptible, progress is being made! He sees his plants mature and begin to reproduce themselves. The early labor of spring gives way to the thrill of the harvest.

And that, I think, is the joy of the preacher's garden. He sees the ancient struggle against sin and Satan played out on a small plot of earth next to a little white church. He dedicates himself to sowing and reaping again. He prays, nourishes, and protects. He waits for God's harvest.

"And let us not lose heart in doing good, for in due time we shall reap a harvest if we do not grow weary." (Galatians 6:9)

⌘ ⌘ ⌘

It is a Mystery to Me

It is February and the florists are looking forward to the grandest day of their sales year. It is estimated that more roses are sold for St. Valentine's Day than any other day of the year. Dozens of the delightful flowers will be purchased for sweethearts, young and old alike. What puts a grin on the grower's face is the price tag, which can range from thirty-six to seventy-five dollars a dozen.

That price is just a little steep for a

practical minded country preacher like me. Thirty-six bucks would buy a lot of Slim-Fast ™ at the local Wal-Mart. ®

I don't think I'm going to get by with thumbing my nose at the rose growers this year, though. Mary and I have now spent twenty-four St. Valentine's Days together, and that comes out to an equal two dozen roses. In that twenty-four years I don't ever recall buying her roses (I would repent in sackcloth and ashes, but they *do* just turn brown and die, you know.).

I did have roses delivered to her once when we were dating. I had no choice. Ours was a rocky, teenaged relationship. I was head-over-heels in love with her. She utterly detested me!

My Mother noticed my dejection. "What's the matter? Girl trouble?"

I shrugged and nodded.

"Don't worry too much about it. Sometimes when a girl says 'no' she really means 'yes.'"

I didn't tell Mom that she hadn't said "no." What she'd said was "phooey!"

So I thought I'd give the Merlin Olson way a try. And do you know what? It worked! One dozen long stemmed beautiful red roses and twelve hard earned gas station dollars went down the drain. But it worked!

I still don't understand why. Maybe it was the mystery of the gift. There wasn't another Sophomore boy in the county dumb enough to have a dozen roses delivered and forget to include a card with his name attached.

"Maybe they are from Doug? Or Billy? I bet Bob sent me these."

By the time she figured out who they really came from I think she would have gone steady with Mr. Rogers. It doesn't really matter. All that matters is that those roses worked. For me.

They were unexpected, and completely out of character for me. Those roses mystified her (and she hasn't had roses from me since, except those I brought home following a funeral I conducted, and I don't think those counted.).

But Mary still talks about the St. Valentine's Day roses she received when she was fifteen.

Like unexpected roses, mysteries pop up in life just for the sake of giving unanticipated joy. And marriage, despite twenty-four years, is something that remains a mystery to me.

Solomon, man of a thousand wives, wrote:

"There are three things too wonderful for me, yes, even four that are a mystery to me. The way of an eagle in the sky. The way of a serpent on a rock. The way of a ship on the sea, and the way of a man with his wife." (Proverbs 30:18).

The way of a man with his wife is a mystery. But thank God, He decided that it "was not good for a man to be alone." Nearly everyone knows the account of how God took a rib from Adam while he slept and created Eve to be his wife.

A Sunday School teacher had explained this creation account to her class, then dismissed them to play. Little Tommy ran and played with abandon. His teacher saw him slumped against the building clutching his side.

"What's the matter, Tommy?"

"Oh, teacher," he gasped. "I think

I'm having a wife!"

There may be more theology in little Tommy's statement than we realize. Perhaps marriage remains mysterious because it is often so painful! Pain may be the reason so many couples find themselves in divorce court. It is often difficult to see past the pain to the magic and mystery of marriage.

I'm no authority on the subject of marriage, but I have learned a lot from my mistakes. Marriage isn't easy, but it can be wonderful.

My own marriage was predicted to end in "dismal failure." I was young. I was broke. Mary had to sell a bottle-fed lamb to raise our marriage license money. To make matters worse, I fainted in the elevator after getting our blood test. (Right about then she would probably have given about anything to have her lamb back!)

To add insult to injury, when we came out of the little Baptist chapel where we were married, we discovered that our young cousins had "decorated" our car. They put a placard on the back of my car that should have read "JUST MARRIED."

Unfortunately, they mis-spelled it, and left the "i" out. I drove away in a car that was emblazoned with the logo "JUST MARRED." How appropriate!

That experience reminds me of the young married couple that wasn't getting along. "You never think!" the young wife scolded her husband. "One more bad decision on your part, and I'm leaving!"

He went out to milk the cow the next morning. The cow kept swishing her tail across his face.

He spied a brick and a piece of rope and thought about tying the brick to the cow's tail. He tied the rope to her tail, but then he hesitated.

"If I tie this brick to the rope on the cow's tail, she might swing it through the air and clobber me in the head. Then my wife will leave me for sure. It's a good thing I thought this through." He took the loose end of the rope and nonchalantly looped it around his neck.

Two days later, from his hospital bed, he candidly commented, "I hadn't been around the barn twice before I realized I had made a terrible mistake."

I've been around the barn a few times myself, but marriage remains a mystery to me. Yet mystery is vitally important to marriage. We may as well accept the challenge and do something unexpected for the one we love.

Be careful though. I heard about an engineer who was working overtime with his colleagues. They discovered that it was his anniversary, and that he hadn't planned anything special for his wife.

"You are among gentlemen!" they said. "You have to take the rest of the day off and do something special for your wife."

They insisted, so he did. He stopped on the way home and bought a big box of chocolates. He stopped again and bought a dozen red roses. Then he went home.

When he entered, his wife whirled around, startled to see him. Then she burst into tears.

"What's the matter, honey?" said the husband, standing in the doorway with his roses and chocolates.

"This has been the worst day of my life!" she sobbed. "This morning, Billy was headed for school and he wrecked his bicycle in the driveway and chipped his front tooth. In my rush to get him to the dentist, I backed over his bike. When I got home, I found I'd left the sink running and the kitchen was flooded."

"And now," she sobbed, "You've come home drunk!"

And marriage isn't the only thing I find mysterious. Raising children is a mystery to me. Some call it "child rearing." I think that the word "rearing" is appropriate. If you do parenting right, you devote as much attention to their "rears" as you do to the rest of them!

I'm not talking about changing diapers, either. I'm talking about old fashioned, Biblical discipline. Proverbs says "He who spares the rod spoils the child." I love my children. I haven't worn out any rods or rears, but my children, now grown, still respect my authority.

My daughter, Sarah, gave me a lesson in dealing with authority once. She wanted to play house, and I was to be the son. I am a little inhibited about things like that, but it meant a lot to Sarah, so I determined to play my part well.

"Go clean your room!" she ordered.

Well, I pretended to have a fit. "I always have to clean the room! Why doesn't my brother have to help?" I whined. "He never has to do anything. It just isn't fair!" (I thought to use a little child psychology, just to show her what she sometimes sounded like.)

Sarah put her little hands on her hips and looked me right in the eye.

"You know," she said, "you're just like your Dad!"

That kind of intelligence in a little kid is confusing to me. They are so unpredictable, so mysterious.

Children want to experience everything they can. Taste, sights, and sounds are tantalizing. Our son Ben ate so much dry dog food when he was a toddler, it wouldn't surprise us today if he started to howl at the moon.

But now, as a teenager, he seems to have lost all his senses! He refuses to try any new dish at the supper table, but turn him loose at the mall candy store, and he will load up on exotic treats like Gummy toads or imitation Tequila flavored Lollipops complete with a little worm inside.

Something is also acutely wrong with his hearing ability.

He was playing a video game the other evening. Loud beeps and squeals permeated our living room.

"Ben, turn that junk down!" I shouted.

No response. I raised my voice to the pitch of the space shuttle taking off. Still no response.

I went to the kitchen and quietly closed the door. I opened the refrigerator and took out a Cola. I popped the tab, but didn't get the can to my lips before Ben yelled, "Will you bring me one too?"

If he can hear, he can't see.

He had been stepping over a pair of dirty socks on his bedroom floor for two weeks. They were in the same place all that time, he never moved them.

"Ben, pick up those socks," I ordered.

"What socks?" The poor boy looked so confused!

"Those socks," I said, pointing.

"Oh," he said. "Those have just been there a few days."

He picked them up. They were so stiff you could have used them like an Australian boomerang!

But just go into his room and try to move something around. Take a stereo cassette from one end of his table and put it on the other end. He'll come to his door and yell, "Who's been into my stuff!"

Marriage and children are mysterious. Yet, they make life interesting and enjoyable.

God didn't leave us in the dark concerning what might have been the greatest mystery of all, though. It is His own love for us, His family, His children.

Now, I don't mind telling you that God's love is mind boggling to a guy who can't figure out his wife and kids. But I know its true, regardless.

Christ has taken up residence in those who trust Him. He has made His home in those who love Him. And perhaps love is what is most significant about St. Valentine's Day.

When we go back in history two thousand years we find Jesus hanging on a cross. He didn't get any roses, but He did

Marriage is a Mystery!

get a crown of thorns.

A placard was nailed above His head, it read "Just Marred." In that image we are confronted with real love.

What is this elusive thing called love?

Maybe the real mystery of marriage and raising children is to be found in the fact that sometimes it hurts. Jesus knew that, too. For Him, the joy of sacrifice was worth the pain of sacrifice.

May it also be with me.

⌘ ⌘ ⌘

A Little Glimpse of Heaven

Heaven is a little hard to understand. Sometimes we do catch a glimpse of it. We may not be looking for it particularly, it just flashes through. I caught a little glimpse of heaven, once.

A gray-haired lady was struggling with several bags in the Knoxville Airport. It wasn't until after I asked her if I could help her that I noticed the infant she carried.

"That's a cute baby. How old is she?" I asked.

"Just three days." The lady smiled.

I carried her things on board and stowed them while she got settled. My seat was two rows back, across the aisle. I watched the lady and the baby and thought the scene a little odd. She was fiftyish, the baby an infant. An airplane flight. It didn't make sense.

I had to change planes in Memphis, and apparently the lady did, too. I asked to help with her bags again. She thanked me.

"Your baby is still sleeping."

"Oh, its not my baby. I'm just delivering her," she explained as I followed her toward the exit.

When we stepped from the D.C.-10 into the waiting area of Gate Eleven, I slowly began to understand.

A frazzled young couple waited. The husband appeared to be physically supporting his trembling wife. Her eyes were filled with tears. Her lips trembled.

Then she saw the baby.

She stripped the baby down to its diaper. With wide eyes she turned the infant this way and that, examining her like a jeweler would a fine diamond. Then she clutched that child to her chest and sat on the floor and wept.

Through tears she asked the lady about the baby's mother. I listened in, mesmerized.

"She's o.k." the Social Worker said.

"She spent this morning with the baby in her hospital room.

"We took some pictures. She said good-bye, then we caught our plane."

This was a little glimpse of heaven! An infant girl closed her eyes in Knoxville and woke up in Memphis in the arms of someone *else* who loved her. Her life was forever, irrevocably changed. What grace, what boundless love.

The couple with their new baby walked out of the airport into a new life.

"My plane returns in an hour."

It was the gray-haired lady. I was still holding her bag.

"Oh," I said as I handed it over. I nodded to the departing couple.

PAGE 37

> **"He predestined us to be adopted as His sons through Jesus Christ, in accordance to His pleasure and will, to the praise of His glorious grace" (Ephesians 1:5).**

"Does that happen often?"

She sighed.

"Not enough. But when it does, it's worth everything."

"Everything," I thought as I watched the trio pass out of sight. "Just like heaven."

⌘ ⌘ ⌘

Of Reunions and Unintentional Sin

"Aren't you hungry? You'd better get something to eat. You're late."

It had been a hectic day. Mary's family reunion had long been planned. But, I forgot (I always do) and scheduled a wedding for the same Saturday morning. Naturally, she was upset. She rightly expected me to be there, but I'd overbooked the calendar again.

"You can go on ahead. The wedding is scheduled for ten o'clock. I think I can be there by noon if I hurry," I said.

It was a small but very nice wedding. Several friends, some family, and a few words from the Good Book would initiate a relationship that I hoped would last a lifetime.

Some hasty handshaking was followed by a long drive to Southeast Kansas for the reunion dinner. And I *was* hungry.

I found the park without difficulty; I'd been there before. On the north side of the main entrance I spotted the reunion crowd. The last of the family was going through the food line beneath the shelter house.

I found a place to park the car and walked briskly to the end of the line. My thought was to fill my plate, and then find my family.

I *really* piled it on. Baked beans, ham, potato salad, fried chicken, green beans.

Then I went to find Mary and our kids. I looked at every picnic table. I looked at families spread out on quilts on the ground. She wasn't there! As a matter of fact, I didn't recognize *anybody!*

The rapidly panicking preacher suddenly discovered he had crashed the Clark family reunion!

"Aren't you going to eat?"

"Uh. . . I'm really not very hungry."

I looked down the hill to the pavilion where the Clark family were still scratching their heads.

"You don't have any distant cousins named Clark, do you?" I asked my puzzled wife.

"No, Why?" She followed my gaze down the hill.

"Well, they make the world's best pecan pie!"

"Chuck! You didn't!"

"Yep," I said. "I sure did."

⌘ ⌘ ⌘

Stuffy Sunday Mornings

Do you remember those stuffy Sunday Mornings when the only thing to stir the air in the Church Sanctuary was a hand held fan bearing an advertisement for the local funeral home? The heat was never a deterrent to worship, though. The Lord was praised, the Word was preached, and the people prayed.

Sometimes I wonder how much life the youth of today are missing out on. One of these days they will be telling their children about "that horrible day back in '96 when the Church air-conditioner went down."

Kids today can't believe that their grandparents could grind their own coffee, churn their own butter, and have nothing colder than a water spring or creek to cool things in.

Grandma cooled the melons in the spring house and sometimes hung the butter in a bucket down the well. Vegetables were gathered with the morning dew still on them and were always crisp and fresh. Chickens and catfish got caught, dressed, and fried almost before they could stop flappin'!

I might not like to go back to the good ol' days for long, but it would be wonderful to turn the clock back long enough for my children to enjoy the aroma of grape blossoms or the country fresh smell of rain on a hot summer day.

Many people claim that we shouldn't live in the past, but I think a good look at the simple joys of our youth might help us to re-evaluate what is important.

In our age of ease there are many values, that though inconvenient, are priceless. Qualities like Integrity. Honor. Patriotism. Prayer. You can't find these in the freezer section of the local grocery and pop them into the micro-wave for a quick snack.

> **In a Bible-believing Church you will discover life changing spiritual truths in a timeless book.**

No, qualities like these are simmered slowly into young lives on a back burner, stirred often by the loving hands of mothers or grandmothers; constantly checked and sampled by fathers and grandfathers.

How can we instill in our children the values that are timeless?

Introduce them to cold lemonade, merry-go-rounds, hot dogs, and the joy of blackberry picking.

Then attend church as a family on Sundays. In a Bible-believing Church you will discover life changing spiritual truths in a timeless book.

⌘ ⌘ ⌘

Light From Grannie's Life

It happened again the other evening. The kids fumbled around in the buffet drawer for our one broken Christmas candle. Then we sat in the dark around the kitchen table and waited for the lights to come on again.

What a bother! Every clock in the house would need reset. The VCR would begin its infernal blinking... blinking. The meat in the freezer might thaw out, and horror of horrors, there would be no television to entertain us tonight!

All of our modern technology had been brought low by one old-fashioned Kansas thunderstorm. I went out to sit on the porch swing and wait for the light to come.

On our Grannie's farm, this storm would not have made a difference. Her old wall clock came from Germany, and you didn't have to plug it in. It was quite a weekly ritual when Grannie Annie took the big brass key and simply wound it up again!

And there wasn't an alarm clock anywhere in her house. I guess if the rooster failed to crow, or the cows forgot to moan for their milking, or the sun refused to shine, it was a good excuse for sleeping in. There wasn't any hurry anyway.

The butter, milk, and eggs were safe in the cold rushing creek. There weren't any light bulbs to burn out, just a few reliable kerosene lamps to keep filled. No electricity. No television. No radio, stereo, or microwave oven.

Just long quiet evenings, an old porch

swing, and hymns to sing.

There was plenty of opportunity to sit, think, rest, listen, and meditate on God's goodness to a poor country widow. Ample time to watch God's thunderstorms roll by.

Up and down the street the lights blinked on again in unison. Mary came to the door.

"Aren't you coming in, honey? *Sixty Minutes* is coming on."

"I don't think so. I think I'll sit here for a little while longer and watch the rain," I said. Mary went back into the house.

"I think I'll sit here a little while longer with Grannie Annie and God's thunderstorm," I thought.

"Listen closely to the thunder of His voice, and the rumbling that goes out of His mouth. Under the whole heaven He lets it loose, and His Lightning to the ends of the earth. After it a voice roars; He thunders with His majestic voice; and He does not restrain the lightnings when His voice is heard. God thunders with His voice wondrously, doing great things which we cannot comprehend." (Job 37:2-5).

⌘   ⌘   ⌘

Lessons From a Well

Grandma and Grandpa lived on the prairie. They had none of the amenities that we find necessary. We took baths in the kitchen, behind the wood stove, in a big old washtub with water drawn from a well. Grandma heated the water in a black cast-iron kettle on the stove. It was a lot of work for her to bathe us. But she didn't mind. She loved us.

That old well down the steps from the back porch had a strange fascination for me. We were city kids. We had running water. I'd go out and peer down the well. It was dark and deep. I'd "holler' down" and listen to my echo reverberate over and over again.

We'd lower the long galvanized bucket into the water, feel it grow heavier and heavier, and then strain together to pull it to the top. We took turns pulling the plunger that sent the water cascading back into the depths of the well.

I got my first taste of reality from that old well. From it I learned that not all of life was for fun. I learned that I was terribly responsible for my actions.

Motivated by a childhood nursery rhyme, I dropped a kitten down the well. "Little Tommy Stout" wasn't there to pull her out again. The reality of what I'd done continued to sink in. In desperation I ran across the warped porch boards calling for Grandma. Tears crept into her weathered eyes when she learned of my deed. They were tears for me.

When Grandpa came in they whispered together. He took me by the hand and led me to the barn, where he got a long piece of barbed wire fence. We went to the well. Grandpa never spoke. He snaked the long wire down the well and quickly whipped it around and around. Then he began a slow retrieve of the wire. He lay the kitten on the ground, unhooked it, and walked away. I was face to face with the reality of my own irresponsibility. The yellow and white striped kitten was dead. I never felt worse. The incident was never mentioned again.

Sin Hurts. There was absolutely nothing I could do to reverse the events. All

> **Sin hurts...All that I could do was determine not to make the same mistake again.**

that I could do was to determine not to make the same mistake again. And I could ask for forgiveness.

Jesus spoke these words to an adulterous woman: "Is there no one who condemns you? Neither do I condemn you. Go your way, but sin no more."

What wonderful advice from a wonderful Savior.

⌘ ⌘ ⌘

Musings on a Screen Door.

It rained this morning, early. I relish the aroma of cool rain on a musty summer morning, so I sat on the porch, about six-thirty, and enjoyed it for a while. It is easy to reminisce in the early morning stillness.

I remember summer things, like fresh fried chicken at a church picnic, or watermelon fights with sneaky, slippery cousins. I remember sand in my hair and the feel of stiff overall straps on my sun burned shoulders.

"Fizzit, click." A soft hissing interrupted my rainy morning musings. I let the porch swing coast to a stop and listened.

"Fizzit, click," the hydraulic cylinder on our front door said again as Mary re-entered our home with the morning paper.

"Fizzit, click? What a whimpy thing for an expensive 'All Weather, Bronze Tone, Insulated, Fully Guaranteed Storm Door' to utter," I thought.

I put the swing back into motion and continued to watch the drizzle. Doors didn't used to sound that way. I think I'd rather have the warm familiarity of an old screen door. I liked the way the door spring used to stretch and squeak out a rusty, but melodious tune that was accompanied by the percussion of a heavy slam.

And I, personally, as a boy had developed screen door slamming into a sport of Olympic proportion. (Momma said that summer was the time of year we slammed the doors we had left open all winter.)

It was the same all up and down our block. A hundred times a day we'd hear a screen door slam followed by the futile motherly cry, "Don't slam the door!"

We never heard "Fizzit, click."

Actually, it was not uncommon to see an eight year old opening the door wide and letting it slam over and over again, out of sheer boredom. He would really get a bang out of it!

I heard about one exasperated mother whose son was always getting into mischief. Finally she asked him, "How in the world do you ever expect to get into heaven?"

The little fellow thought it over. "I'll just run in and out, and keep slammin' the door until St. Peter says what you say."

The mother was startled. "What do I say?" she asked, puzzled.

"You say, 'For heaven's sake, Jimmy either come in or stay out!'" he answered.

"Fizzit click. Fizzit, click." Not enough racket to perturb a Mom, let alone St. Peter. I got up and went over to see if there was any way to slam the thing for old times sake. Mary came to the door.

"What's the matter? Is there something wrong with the door?"

How could I tell her? "No," I said simply. "There isn't anything wrong with the door." I sighed and went in to get another cup of coffee.

"Fizzit, click."

⌘ ⌘ ⌘

Leonard's Pond

I felt absolutely ill as I stood on the weed-infested shore of a moss green pool of stagnant water that Leonard had described as a "stock pond." It was not what I had envisioned at all, and I was sick about it.

"Ja," he had said. "Eben she's got enough vater in her for a goot baptism."

I had imagined good, *clean* water that any self respecting cow would drink from with gusto. But the only cow to be seen was a dirty gray cow on the opposite shore. She had mud on her, and not just a little, but muddy slime that extended from her hooves all the way up past the hocks of her legs.

I had fire in my eyes and I looked for Leonard. He was basking in the pride of the area's first baptism in a few years.

"Ja! And she vus on my property; ja she vus; right ober dere in my berry own 'stock pond'. Es goot, eh?"

"Simply vunderful." I said to myself.

I was determined to make the best of it, though. How excited I had been when Frank burst from his pew! I had never seen anyone respond to an invitation so quickly. Linda, his wife, had followed closely behind him. They both came and knelt at the prayer rail, weeping. Soon, their two teenaged daughters joined them, all weeping. I dismissed the service. What else could I do? The four of them were weeping, and none of them could speak.

The congregation sang "All to Jesus I surrender" as I waded into the stagnant pool. They had waited patiently in the vestibule while I counseled with the Smith family, who recovered sufficiently to make their decisions known. Our church's baptistry didn't work. Leonard volunteered his stock pond. "Ja!"

The water did not reach my waist. I turned to go back to shore and discovered I had created a "chocolate" wake. The water was like warm cocoa only slightly cooled.

Flies buzzed the surface of the water, and I knew why. It stank. With each step I labored to pull my feet from the mud. I thought about the cows, who until recently, had been cooling themselves in my baptistry. As I struggled to shore I wondered if anyone had ever been baptized in a septic tank.

Linda was first, lucky woman. I led her into the water. She was beaming. We struggled along together to the center of the pond. Not finding any deeper water, I asked Linda to get down on her knees.

"It will probably be more spiritual

that way, anyhow," I thought to myself.

I asked Linda for her confession of faith and then plunged her beneath the water's surface.

I was amazed to hear what sounded like two muffled rifle shots discharged beneath the surface. Instantly I realized it was the sound of Linda's knees popping, and jerked her to the surface.

She was still beaming. Ooze was in her long blond hair, instantly changed brunette. Chocolate rivulets of water ran down her face and dripped into the watery grave.

I tried to help her up. To my horror, she would not budge. Sunk she was, up to her thighs in mud. I looked anxiously to the shore for assistance. The little congregation stared back expectantly. Perhaps the new preacher wasn't finished yet.

I braced myself and put both arms under her arm and tried to lift. I strained with all my might. Leonard grinned broadly from shore.

Slowly she began to budge. I was just about to breath a sigh of relief when the mud in the bottom of the pond breathed its own sigh instead. It was a long, *long*, drawn out disgusting noise. . . . . a *schluuuupp* that would not quit.

My face flashed as hot as the tepid water. The *schluuuupp* repeated itself as Linda's other leg came free, and she staggered toward the edge of the water.

> # . . .it is a Good and Loving God . . .Who can Wash Away Sin.

My back ached, and my ego was flat.

One by one the others joined me in the swamp on Leonard's farm, and the water churned progressively blacker with each baptism. Frank was the last to be immersed and he hauled me quickly, but not noiselessly, from the mud. We all stood on the bank together, slimy, but happy while the congregation sang "Now I belong to Jesus."

How I had prayed for my first ministry to be successful, and my first baptism to be perfect.

It was, in retrospect.

The Smith family had learned the joy of obedience in a way they would never forget. And God had taught me a lesson in humility that I would always remember.

The words of Ananias to Saul of Tarsus rang in my ears: "And now, why do you delay? Arise and be baptized, and wash away your sins, calling on His name" (Acts 22:16).

> *"and now, why do you delay?"*

Surely it is a good and loving God who can use a bungling young preacher and a pondful of muddy water to wash away sin.

"Ja! Es goot, eh?"

"Es goot, Leonard. Es very goot."

⌘ ⌘ ⌘

One of Life's Little Lessons

Claude (pronounced "clod") moved to my boyhood home town the summer following our Sixth Grade year. He was from the Eastern hill country of Oklahoma, and knew lots of stuff us city-slickers didn't.

Claude knew about "chawin' tobaccy," and I was fascinated. It seemed pretty grown up to walk around and spit. I encouraged him to teach me, and he quickly agreed. There really wasn't much to it, just pack the stuff into your cheek, and when the juice became overwhelming, spit. That's it.

I had been doing a good job with it, too. Hot July days were spent roamin' and spittin'. Fishin' and spittin'. Just sittin' and spittin.' Now that was one mighty fine way to spend a summer!

One swell day Claude and I decided to add another act to our repertoire; swimmin' and spittin.' It might have worked out, had it not been a particularly hot day. And it was a long hike across Mrs. Ansley's plowed field to our favorite swimmin' hole on the Little Arkansas River. But we were set on it, so we walked, talked, sweat, and of course, spit.

We were almost to the river when I tripped over a clod (pronounced Claude), fell, and swallowed; chewing tobacco, spit, and all.

You haven't lived until you've swallowed a big chaw of Red Indian! But, at that moment it really didn't seem too bad.

Until, that is, I'd swallowed a generous portion of river water. And then that Indian pictured on the package cover began to do a little war dance in my twelve year old tummy.

My head began to spin, my eyes burned, and my knees buckled. Before I knew it, well, lets just say the boys were clearing out of the swimmin' hole in a hurry.

It sure was a long slow crawl back

> **"Whatever a Man Sows, this he will also Reap"**

home on a hot day in July.

"Why, you're just absolutely green!" Momma said as I wilted into the sofa.

"What's the matter?"

I feebly pointed to my stomach, saying nothing.

She smiled a knowing smile, disappeared into the kitchen, then came right back.

"Open up," she commanded as she poured a thick liquid from a big black bottle into a tablespoon.

"Even a big boy like you can stand a good dose of cod liver oil from time to time," she grinned.

She knew. What Intuition! I don't know how she knew, but she knew. I couldn't tell the truth, I had to take the cure.

"Do not be deceived, God is not mocked; for whatever a man sows, this he will also reap" (Galatians 6:7, New American Standard Version).

⌘ ⌘ ⌘

A Memory of the Fourth of July

You know you are in trouble when:
a. The Cocker Spaniel is having conniption fits under your father's bed.
b. Your kid brother has vanished in the blink of an eye.
c. Your father is shrieking on the front porch in broad daylight dressed only in his boxer shorts.
d. All of the above.

It was the Fourth of July, and Mike and I were celebrating our independence by forlornly pouting on the front porch.

All of the neighborhood kids were lighting fire-crackers up and down the street. Not us. We were forbidden. We looked forward to the Fourth of July with nearly the same enthusiasm as Christmas. We had a big brown grocery bag filled with fire-crackers. But we were forbidden to shoot them.

"But, Momma! we've waited soooo long!"

"You boys know your father had to work the late shift last night. There will be no fireworks until he is up." End of discussion.

Wendy, our nervous Cocker Spaniel, moped with us on the steps. Mike looked her over and figured we could slip a fire-cracker through the metal ring on her collar. He figured when we lit it, she would run down the block, and it would explode so far away that no one would ever know we did it.

"She might even like it so much she'll want to do it again," said Mike.

I hesitated.

"It will wiggle out and fall on the ground down by the Palmer's house," Mike reasoned. "I'm *sure* she'll like it."

Well, I'll do just about *anything* to keep my dog happy.

I think the mutt sensed the plan and plotted revenge. At any rate, the second the fuse was lit, the dog raced through the torn place in the screen door and scrambled under our sleeping father's bed.

A mere half-second later I heard the explosion, the dog was howling, Mike had disappeared, and I was joined on the front porch by a semi-nude maniac father.

Needless to say, our celebrating was over for the day. Fire-crackers were confiscated. Michael was found. There was a dad to appease and a dog to calm (maybe it was the other way around?). And of course, we had to plead our case in Mom's court.

Eventually we came to know that real freedom is not to be found in stretching or breaking the rules. We can't even re-write them. Real independence comes when we are completely dependent upon the rules. Our country's rules. Our parents' rules. Our God's rules. True freedom finds us when we respect the rules.

I'd say that's a pretty good lesson for the Fourth of July.

⌘ ⌘ ⌘

Mothers Deserve a "Thank You"

Three rosy-cheeked kids promised Mom a special Mother's Day, complete with breakfast in bed. No, she must not help, though from the noise in the kitchen Mother wondered if some assistance wasn't necessary.

In the kitchen, Chris, Ben, and Sarah got out three pots, two frying pans, a double boiler, three mixing bowls, a chopping board, six measuring spoons, and eight serving dishes. Mom was delighted. She said it was the best JELLO she ever tasted!

For children, Mother's day is a wonderful opportunity to learn to say, "Thanks, Mom."

Sometimes Mothers are the last to hear the word "Thanks," even though they offer us our first human relationship on

> **"Her children shall rise up and call her blessed."**

earth. A cartoon once showed a psychologist talking to a female patient.

"Let's see," he said. "You spend fifty percent of your energy on your job, fifty percent on your husband, and fifty percent on your children. I think I see your problem."

Some moms can really identify with that lady's predicament.

I like the story about the little four and six year old boys who presented their Mom with a house plant. It was especially nice because they purchased it with their own money from the local florist.

The older child lamented, "We wanted to get you a great big bouquet. But it was too expensive. It had a real nice ribbon on it that said 'rest in peace,' and we thought it would be perfect because you are always asking for a little peace so you can rest."

Most moms would love to have "a little peace so they can rest," though they may not find it in this life.

The ministry of Moses, the nobility of Samuel, and the compassion of Jesus were largely dependent upon the influences of their godly mothers.

Thus it has always been. Mother is the first teacher and the greatest influence on her children. She deserves her day.

"Her children shall rise up and call her blessed" (Proverbs 13:20).

⌘ ⌘ ⌘

In Search of Rest

A sunrise in the Ozark Mountains is a soothing thing. It's restful and full of beauty. A cup of coffee, God Almighty, and an Ozark sunrise. It is hard to improve on that.

Everything is serene. Quiet. Those I love the most are still asleep in our little camper. Safe. Serene.

Very soon, though, the city of Branson will awaken in the valley below us. Automobiles, mopeds, and go-carts will roar to life again. Steam trains and tour buses. Tourists.

We will get up, pack our gear and hit the tortoise crawl, bumper to bumper in search of vacation. Another day of map misunderstandings. More McMuffins.® More back seat battles and amusement parks.

While I considered all this a squirrel bounced to a nearby branch to consider me. I sipped my coffee and told that squirrel what I considered the truth.

"What I'd really like is another week on the farm. That would be a *real* vacation. The morning sun would peek through weather bleached curtains and find me sleeping on a home-made chicken feather bed.

"I would wake again to the sound of rattling cook stove lids and the aroma of fried country ham and hot gravy.

"I would like to go out on the porch again and hear a symphony of clucking hens accompanied by the percussion of hog feeder lids.

"I would trade a barefoot run down a dusty country road for any amusement park ride this world could offer.

"I would eat hot buttermilk biscuits and fresh blackberries.

"I would re-explore the dark wooded trails of childhood memory."

The squirrel just watched me and blinked. He couldn't understand. A robin rustled in the thick fallen oak leaves for a grub. A car door slammed. A motor revved to life. My reverie was over.

Vacation. We've come so far now in search of one I doubt if we can ever find our way back to the place where we left it. Every person I know will keep searching for peace and rest. I pray we find it, if not in this life certainly in the next.

"Come to me, all who are weary and heavy laden, and I will give you rest" (Matthew 11:28).

Those are the words of Jesus.

Thank you, Jesus, for the promise of rest.

⌘ ⌘ ⌘

We Got By With Murder

"Class, I need to run an errand. I'll be out of the building for several minutes. While I'm gone I expect you to behave yourselves. You can work on your reading

PAGE 74

assignment for tomorrow."

With that announcement our new Fourth Grade teacher was gone. Such trust! Such Naivete! I shot from my seat and peeked down the hall. I watched as she disappeared around the corner at the far end. It was party time!

A guard was quickly appointed to watch for our teacher's return. Then we ran around the room and pestered the girls. They remained in their seats, they always did what they were supposed to.

But we threw erasers. We made a frantic dash to our desks when the lookout squealed, "She's coming!"

We were cherubs. . . innocent. Diligent students at work. It really didn't surprise me that we got away with it. After all, our teacher was *really* old (37), and

> "Be sure, your sin will find you out."

apparently, not too bright. She said nothing when she righted her overturned chair. She didn't notice the chalk dust eraser rectangles that peppered the

PAGE 75

blackboard.

We got away with murder!

That's what I thought, anyway, until I got the letter.

It was from her, my Fourth Grade teacher, after all of these years. She wanted to know if I was the same Chuck that had been in her class. She wrote that she had enjoyed some of my newspaper articles.

She informed me that she had always suspected I had some leadership (she called it "ringleader") potential.

"Each year," she explained, "during the first week of school, I always use a little ruse to find out who the troublemakers are. I excuse myself from class, walk casually down the hall, then dart out the door and make a mad dash to my classroom window. After spying for a while, I know just exactly who to watch out for. That year it was you."

Man, those Fourth Grade teachers are sneaky!

"Be sure your sin will find you out" (Numbers 32:23, New American Standard Version).

⌘ ⌘ ⌘

Please Pass the Biscuits

When Jesus was in the wilderness, fasting after his baptismal service, He grew hungry. Satan was "Johnny on the Spot" and tempted Christ to turn stones into bread. Christ could have done it, too! But He didn't. Christ always chose sacrifice over shortcuts.

I don't know of anyone, these days, who could turn stones into bread. My wife did just the opposite once, though. She turned biscuits into stones. The boys and I tried to eat them. We just couldn't! They reminded us of that old Army song:

"The biscuits in the Army, they say are mighty fine, one fell off a table, and killed a pal of mine!"

Mary tried to throw them out and the birds wouldn't even eat them. Finally, the boys carried them into the garage and painted them with a can of blue spray paint. They played hockey with them for several months.

What made my wife's biscuits turn into stone? Just a shortcut. When you get the ingredients wrong nothing turns out right.

> **"Man does not live by bread alone..."**

In our day it doesn't look like we're getting life's ingredients quite right. So many people want to take the shortcuts. In the news of late we've all read or heard about those who take shortcuts.

Someone uses a gun or a knife to forcefully take what they want, or short circuit justice.

Somebody pays the bodyguard of an Olympic hopeful to brandish an iron rod.

And if you've visited a book store lately, you'll find a bevy of "self help" books. Titles read: *101 Quick and Easy Ways to Success in* _____ (You fill in the blank). Stones into bread. What a tempting concept.

Christ Jesus didn't teach us that concept, though. When Satan tempted Him with the easy way, He chose the *Via Dolorosa,* the "Way of Sorrows."

He knew that there are no shortcuts to the spiritual life. There are no quick and easy ways to a wonderful marriage. Certainly, there are no effortless ways to the top of one's class or business. The way of Christ is the way of sacrifice.

So when the tempter comes with all of his media hype, tell him you are not interested in any shortcuts.

Tell him "Man does not live by bread alone, but on every word that comes from the mouth of God" (Matthew 4:4, New International Version).

And please, pass the biscuits.

⌘ ⌘ ⌘

A Lesson Learned and Remembered

Greg and I were in search of a science project of import when, one fateful day, a fly buzzed into Greg's open carton of milk. Firm believers in the concept that most significant discoveries are made by accident, we immediately recognized the potential for revelation. I watched the clock while Greg held the insect submerged with his fork. Exactly two minutes and eighteen seconds elapsed from the time of submersion until the last twitch.

Together we corroborated the fact that the fly was dead. Greg nonchalantly flipped it out onto the cafeteria table. I casually used the salt shaker to give the fly a decent burial. The girls at our table looked away with disdain and disgust. Greg and I smiled at each other.

Refocusing our attention on the salt pile, we were mutually amazed to see some movement. We watched as the fly arose, Phoenix like, from the salt. We had witnessed a genuine resurrection.

My colleague and I put our heads together and soon deduced that the salt had absorbed the moisture from the fly's body, thus reviving him.

We wrote, and humbly submitted for our teacher's consideration, a scholarly dissertation on the diverse ramifications of our recent postulations.

Mr. Grubb was not impressed. It was obvious to us that he had failed to see the significance of our recent discovery. He could not have been thinking, for it was all too clear to us: Simply put a dump truck filled with salt on every beach in the country. If someone drowned, help was only seconds away.

The girls in our class were amused to discover that we had failed. Again.

Needless to say, we were under extreme pressure to redeem ourselves. Like true scientists, we determined to "Try, try again."

Having recently dissected a frog in class we felt confident about moving on to bigger and better things. We thought it might be significant to the field of anatomy if we were to chloroform a living creature, explore its innards, close the incision and release the animal relatively uninjured. Greg thought Suzy Johnston would make a good project. I dissuaded him.

We decided on the old yellow cat that waited patiently by the playground door for scraps of food the girls brought it from the cafeteria. Our plan caused such an outcry of indignation from the fairer sex, however, that our principal quickly extinguished our enthusiasm for the project. The girls smiled smugly at us.

Providentially, Greg was able to procure a fine specimen, a dead rabbit, from the highway in front of his house. He brought it to school in a brown paper bag the next day. During our free period we began a painstaking autopsy of the unfortunate creature. Our progress was slow.

To alleviate the tension and stress of our arduous experimentation, my colleague and I planned a momentary diversion that involved the cat.

We caught her quickly, and in a very short time, had transformed her into a creature beyond recognition.

We mummified her. With the help of the school's first aid kit we wrapped up Old Yeller' like the victim of the worst sort of horrible accident. Her head was wrapped with gauze, one eye covered, and with an ear pinned down against her head.

In our haste and excitement we had wound her hind legs up together. Greg was nearly delirious as I applied rabbit blood to the outer wrappings of gauze for effect. We released the cat into the hall just as the bell rang signalling the change of classes.

The following chaos was extraordinary.

Books flew as coeds screamed and headed for the sanctuary of the Girls Room.

Our creation hop-loped down the hall, front claws furiously flailing, fighting for traction. The cat became suddenly frightful to look upon, a three legged cyclops of a meowing, squalling mummy.

We had created a monster. She was out of control, tearing and biting and chewing at herself, her one glazed eye trying to pierce the darkness of her terror. She could not understand. She could not escape. She was powerless to help herself.

Greg was slumped against the wall in mirth. I felt guilty. I carried the cat to the door and gently released her.

It has been twenty-five years, but I saw that cat again today in an exquisitely beautiful woman in a soft yellow dress.

She was in a wheelchair at the mall. Valiantly and violently this lady of infinite courage fought against her cerebral palsy and the ramp which was her obstacle to another level.

In my mind I relived my Jr. High experience again. I saw Greg slumped against the lockers, laughing at this creature of God bound against her will in the wrappings of misfortune.

I could almost hear screams and see people fleeing in horror from something they feared and misunderstood.

Once again I could see the friendly, trusting, soft yellow cat as it lay against the lockers, sides heaving, waiting for release.

Her quiet "meow" said, "Help me. Please."

I didn't hesitate. God had prepared me for this moment. I pushed the beautiful lady to the top of the ramp.

I was suddenly a school boy again.

I felt awkward.

I shoved my hands deep into my pockets.

I hung my head and shuffled my feet.

She smiled at me warmly.

I returned her smile, grateful for the opportunity God had given me to care.

⌘　⌘　⌘

Time To Give Thanks

Row upon row of canned goods sparkled like diamonds in Grandma's kitchen cupboard. With wealth like that, it was hard for us city kids to believe that our grandparents were poor.

She lined her buffet with pies. The smell of nutmeg, cinnamon, and pumpkin was heavy in the air. (Wouldn't it be great to have another slice of her pie right now?)

Freshly pressed apple cider glimmered in a cut glass pitcher on her round oak table. If you wanted some, you could help yourself.

"They're only little once," Grandma would say when your mother protested.

The turkey was roasting in the oven and the aroma of baked dressing was enough to drive any kid wild.

Grandpa carried in a washtub of

> **"It is a good thing to give thanks to the Lord."**

potatoes that he had raked from the straw under the house. At the slam of a car door, excited children would race across the parlor to press chubby noses against the frosty window pane, excited by the arrival of eight more cousins.

Yes, Thanksgiving was a cornucopia of sights, sounds, and tantalizing fragrances.

But when Grandpa took his place at the head of the table and folded his hands to pray, we knew that it was also a time to give thanks. What a wonderful thing it is to know, even as a small child, that someone you deeply love is grateful for *you*. To hear *your* name mentioned in a prayer of thanksgiving to an almighty God is an experience that a youngster is not soon to forget.

Grandpa let God, and all of us, know that he was thankful for us. Our hearts should ache for all of those children who do not have the affirmation of the love of a grateful family.

Thanksgiving is a time to give thanks. Our Grandparents' wealth had nothing to do with the amount of money they had in the Stockman's Grange Bank. Their wealth consisted in what they had that they were willing to give away.

Grandma and Grandpa were willing to give us everything they had. They were very rich, and so are we, because of them.

"It is a good thing to give thanks to the Lord" (Psalm 92:1, New American Standard Version).

⌘ ⌘ ⌘

Upended By Foolish Pride

Hey, let's be honest. When you are in High School, the nicer your car, the nicer your girlfriend. That's the way it works, right? It is an unwritten law. "Thou, foxy chick, shalt not ride, nor be seen in a 1969 Ford station wagon."

They won't be seen in one, either. This is a fact of life tantamount to the laws of the Medes and Persians. *Real* babes ride in *Real* cars. When I went to school if you didn't have a set of cool wheels you could just forget about going out with girls.

So I had spent all of my money getting a cool set of wheels. I was on the verge of dating a real babe. Judy. Yes, Judy. She wore the shortest skirts in High School, and guess who she asked to give her a ride home? Me. She didn't have to ask twice.

My conscience was giving me a little struggle as we went to the car. Mrs. Frinkle's Sunday School lesson was ringing in my ears.

"Sometimes pride will make you act foolishly," she had said. "It's foolish pride that makes you want everyone to think that you are graceful or smooth."

"What did she know?" I thought to myself. It didn't matter that she had asked me to read from Obadiah 1:3-4:

"The arrogance of your heart has deceived you, you who live in the clefts of the rock, in the loftiness of your dwelling place, who say in your heart, 'Who will bring me down?' Though you build high like the eagle, though you set your nest among the stars, 'From there I will bring you down,' declares the Lord" (New American Standard Version).

All that mattered to me was Judy.

I had long anticipated a beautiful Fall day like this. My 1953 Chevy was polished and prime, a labor of love. Just yesterday I had installed the finishing touch. Bucket seats. Red leather, from a 1966 salvage yard Thunderbird. The whole school seemed to be watching as Judy climbed in.

We rumbled across the black topped parking lot to the stop sign at the entrance to the street.

"Vroom, vroom." I revved up the motor to get attention. Every eye was glued to that Chevy, Judy, and me. I realized I was the envy of every boy in the school. Judy was pristinely poised on her red leather throne. I grinned at the guys, popped the clutch, and squealed down the street.

I turned to smile at Judy, but to my amazement, she was not there! She had been replaced by two inverted, chalky white, chubby legs that were aimed heavenward and were vigorously flailing back and forth in space!

I was really astonished. I traced those pale chubby legs to their source and immediately realized that they were attached to the backside of Judy.

I had set her seat in place, but had forgotten to bolt it to the floor.

> **"Pride goes before destruction, and a haughty spirit before a fall."**

There she was, my foxy babe, in all her glory. I screeched to the curb, ran around the car, and helped her out.

She stomped off towards home, never to ride with me again. I collapsed on the curb and laughed, and laughed, and laughed.

Judy and I learned some valuable lessons that day.

She learned to never ride with me again.

I saw a side of Judy I had never seen before, and learned that some things are not what they appear to be.

The prestige I had desired and eagerly sought from my car and Judy was pretty much worthless. What I had done was vain.

Judy, I learned, was not the goddess on a pedestal we thought she was. She was a vulnerable human being, and so was I.

I learned so much that day. On the way home I remembered more of my dowdy Sunday School teacher's lesson on foolish pride. Judy's tumble gave new meaning to the words of Proverbs 16:18:

"Pride goes before destruction, and a haughty spirit before a fall" (New American Standard Version).

Yes, I learned much that day. No matter how hard I try, I know it will be impossible for me to forget the lessons of that day.

Important truths...

"Hey you guys! Did you know that Judy wears a girdle?"

⌘ ⌘ ⌘

Things That Didn't Happen

In just a few minutes time all of us could list a number of things we are thankful for. As a matter of fact, the word "thankful" comes from an old Anglo-Saxon word, "thinkful." If we'll think, we'll give thanks.

Most of us would immediately reflect on the blessings we've *received*. But did you ever think about the things that could have happened, but *didn't?*

I am delighted for a couple that Mary and I know who just had another baby boy. They already have three children, the youngest in the Fourth Grade. What makes their story extraordinary is that, eight years ago, feeling their family was complete, they opted for a surgical method of birth control. Surprise! I'm happy that they are happy. But I am thankful that it didn't happen to me.

    I'm sure that you see what I mean. There are plenty of things that *didn't* happen that ought to cause us to give thanks.

    I *wasn't* in a plane crash. I *didn't* lose any money in the stock market. My wife *didn't* get pregnant.

    When I think about thankfulness in this way, I see that being thankful necessitates keeping events in a proper perspective.

    Perhaps you heard the story about the college girl who finally wrote a letter home to her parents. She wrote:

    "Dear Mom and Dad. I'm sorry that I haven't written in a while, but all of my stationery was destroyed in the dormitory fire.

    "I'm out of the hospital now, and the doctor says there is a good chance that my eyesight will be restored.

    "While I have been out of the dorm I have been living with a young rock musician named Bill. He seems like a nice guy, and there is a chance that you could become grandparents real soon.

"Love, your daughter, Beth.

"P.S. I'm not blind, there was no fire, and I'm not pregnant. However, I did receive a D- in Algebra, and I wanted you to receive this news in the proper perspective."

See what I mean? It could always be worse. We should keep all of life's events in perspective.

Mary has a friend that I'll call Ann. Ann was having some difficulty with the circulation in her legs. Her doctor prescribed that she get a pair of "Job's Hose." (Job was a biblical man who suffered much. Maybe the hose are named after him?).

Anyway, these hose are special made, custom fit, extremely elastic pantyhose. They fit so snugly that it takes several minutes of vigorous struggling to inch them on.

Ann wedged herself into hers in the dressing room of the orthopedic shop. It took her a long time, and she complained that they "didn't feel quite right."

"Don't worry, everybody says that. That is the way they are supposed to feel. You'll get used to them," she was assured. Ann finished dressing and drove across town to do some shopping. I'll let Ann tell you the rest of her story:

"I was pushing the cart down the aisle and those pantyhose suddenly snapped back like a rubber band that had been stretched too tight!

"The hose shot down around my ankles and yanked my slacks down with them! I was just standing there with my pants down!

"I would have made a run for it if my purse hadn't been covered up with groceries in the cart.

"The only thing I could do was wrestle out of those hose and put my slacks back on."

Ann could laugh about it, but I'm pretty sure I couldn't. I'm just thankful that it didn't happen to me.

"All things work together for good for those who love the Lord and are called according to His purposes" (Romans 8:28).

⌘ ⌘ ⌘

Thanksgiving Cornucopia

On the front porch little boys in heavy coats push green and yellow toy tractors across weathered gray floor boards.
Long legged men in striped overalls step over them to lean against ornamental

white porch pillars.

"No smoking in the house!" So they visit outside and tamp hand carved pipes.

The tractors chug and the pipes puff.

Cherry Blend and loud talk, politics swirl and mix.

"Did you hear the one about.....?"

Guffawing. Whispered punch lines.

In the kitchen crisp aprons rustle over frilly dresses.

Limp dolls are clutched and crushed by fat cheeked little girls who keep getting in the way.

Feminine faces flush over the banging lids of boiling potato pots.

"No smoking in the house!" The cry is repeated.

A dark bronze turkey politely waits on its platter.

"Let me tell you what little Amy did." Laughter.

"Say Momma. Say Momma," a little girl commands. Her doll obediently responds.

The women talk about chickens, laying and frying. Sewing. Having babies.

Lisa pats her swelling tummy. Ellana

Marie will be her first.

At the table the fragrances of nutmeg

> **The Lord whispers, "You're welcome."**

and pumpkin meet and mingle.

There is some backslapping, some nudging and poking, fussing and shuffling as the family gathers and presses around the table.

Jamie grabs a handful of cranberry sauce that oozes between her fingers.

Grandma and Grandpa, brothers and sisters, aunts and uncles. Cousins.

There is a brief hesitant silence, then a simple heartfelt prayer.

"Thank you, Good Lord, for the bounty of Thy blessing. Thank you for this family. Our family. Amen."

In heaven the Good Lord looks down and grins as Jamie smears the sauce down the front of her frilly little dress.

Mischievous Chris pours dill pickle juice in unsuspecting cousin Amy's tea glass and the Lord chuckles.

He has seen, He has heard, He is present.

In the midst of all that commotion, the Lord looks, and He smiles.

The Lord whispers, "You're welcome."

⌘ ⌘ ⌘

The Fire is Out

Football is back in fashion and winter has begun to wrap us in her coat of white. The leaves on our pumpkin vines have long been brown. In a very short time the seasons will spiral around, but for now we're only interested in backing up to a warm hearth.

Nothing quite beats a blazing fire on

a frigid day. In one of the homes we owned there was a magnificent fireplace. It was built from massive cut limestone blocks, with an ornate carved dark oak mantel. It was the focal point of our home, Mary delighted in decorating that mantel for every season.

The unusual thing about our fireplace wasn't the cozy, decorated charm it added to our home. The amazing thing was how warm it made our visitors feel. Many arriving guests on a cold winter evening made their way into the dining room to wash their hands in the cheerful glow of our fireplace.

They seemed to enjoy it so much that, frankly, we hesitated to point out that our fireplace was a phony. It had long been boarded up to keep the raccoons out. As time progressed it had exchanged burning wood for an expensive spinning color wheel behind ceramic logs.

There was plenty of action, light, and color, and the red cellophane strips flickered in a fan generated breeze, but there was no heat.

No heat. Some modern day churches might be accused of the same infraction. In our quest for bigger and better and more ornate fireplaces we may have forgotten about the heat. We advertise fire, but any warmth generated may be purely psychological. The blower may be blowing , but the fire

> **No heat. Some modern day churches might be guilty of the same infraction.**

may be out.

I'd wager that when this old world of ours gets really cold we'd trade all of the glitz and glitter of cellophane for a little real heat.

A dirty black parlor stove, squat and fat and full of fire would be a welcome friend on a frosty night. It might not seem like much by today's standards, but its square glass eyes would glow with delight as it welcomed each visitor from the cold.

We ought to remember that a little real fire, in even a modest stove can do much to warm a freezing world. The same thing is true of our churches.

⌘ ⌘ ⌘

Watching the Fire Spread

My good friend Harvey was telling me how he used to get his 1927 Ford Coupe going on cold winter days.

"I'd take an old gunny sack and light it on fire and push it under the oil pan. It's a wonder I never burned the old car up, but that was just enough heat to get the danged car going."

I wonder if that would work on people? No, I wouldn't burn anybody at the stake, but some people do need a fire lit under them.

The story is told of a small town fire chief who was standing amid the ashes of a burned out church. The pastor saw him there.

"This is the first time I ever saw *you* in church," kidded the pastor.

"This is the first time I ever saw this church on fire," said the fire chief. That may be a sad reflection of our times.

> **We need a baptism of the Holy Spirit and Fire.**

Every Christian church *ought* to be on fire for God.

According to Matthew 3:11, Jesus' arrival would bring about a "baptism of the Holy Spirit and fire." We need that heat in the modern day church. We need the fire of the Holy Spirit promised by Christ.

On these cold winter days I know I could use a little help in getting up and getting started for God. What would it be like if all of us were to tap into the most powerful energy source in the universe?

We should be united in our prayers for Holy Spirit Fire. A consuming and illuminating fire. A warming fire. We need sermons on fire, choirs afire, church members on fire, prayer meetings and Bible studies afire.

If you pray for fire, be ready for it to come and spread. In 1871 an old woman known as Mother O'Leary was milking a cow by lantern light in Chicago. You know the rest of that story! Let's do what we can to get a fire of revival lit, and God will do the rest.

We'll light it, God will fan it into flame, and then we'll watch it spread.

⌘ ⌘ ⌘

Grandpa's Coffee

Grandpa boiled his coffee in a battered tin pan on the top of his old stove. It was strong and black. The wonderful aroma of Arbuckle coffee on a frosty winter morning is sill a pleasant memory to me. The only problem was that no one could drink the stuff. Except Grandpa. He just added more coffee to the grounds and kept it boiling all day long.

We bought him a nice stainless steel percolator once. He promptly threw away the "innards," lost the cord, and continued to boil his coffee on the stove. We learned that he liked it best that way. Strong and unadulterated. If we complained, he had a standard answer.

"If it's too strong for you, just water it down a little."

We did. A lot.

The world still operates on Grandpa's coffee formula. "Just water it down a little." And that includes what is being done to the gospel, as well.

So much water has now been added that some claim Hell is no longer hot; Sin isn't bad; Salvation isn't sweet, and Jesus Christ is no longer the only way to heaven.

Yes sir, there are lots of folks who are content to sip from a lukewarm cup. Jesus must desire more from His disciples than that!

"So then because thou art lukewarm, and neither cold nor hot, I will spew thee out of my mouth" (Revelation 3:16, King James Version).

When you drink your coffee tomorrow, drink it any way you like it. But when the gospel is taught or preached, demand it in all its strength.

⌘ ⌘ ⌘

Nitcher's Grocery Store

"Dad, I'm bored."

I don't relate well to the boredom small town kids now claim to experience. But, I don't relate well to Ninja Turtles ® or hundred dollar Nike ® shoes, either.

I do know about hoola-hoops, canvas basketball shoes and rocking back and forth in the Buick's big steering wheel while Mom shopped inside Nitcher's.

Nothing could banish Saturday morning boredom like the opportunity to go down town. I'd like to walk up to the big, black painted screen door and pull on the cold metal Nehi ® Grape Soda handle again; to feel the heft of that door and listen to it slam behind me as Mrs. Nitcher eyed me warily from behind the counter.

It was a special treat just to be allowed inside!

Inside were nickel candy bars the size of shoe boxes. There were exotic oranges, radiant bananas, brilliant apples. Long aisles for strolling and grapes for snitching. Noses were pressed against the cold glass meat case full of bologna, salami, and cheese.

I remember discreetly checking the flour sacks, just like Momma taught me, wary of weevils (I always hoped to find some, though I never did).

At eye level I'd watch the groceries slide down the long counter to be tallied and sacked.

And then came a mysterious, magical question. In those days nobody asked, "Paper or Plastic?" We got a bag or a box.

The question of those days was "Cash, or charge?" Mrs. Nitcher would smile.

We would charge. Everybody did. The ticket, once signed, would disappear

> **"Owe nothing to any man, except to love one another; for he who loves his neighbor fulfills the law."**

into a cigar box to be picked up at an undetermined later date. No questions asked.

For a wild and wide eyed boy there was fun, friendliness, and food to be found at Nitcher's Grocery Store. But there was also faith.

It was faith in your fellow man. Faith that you could trust others to do what they said they would do.

Faith and giant nickel candy bars.

"Owe nothing to any man except to love one another; for he who loves his neighbor fulfills the law" (Romans 13:8).

⌘ ⌘ ⌘

I Heard an Angel's Voice

I was young and hadn't been a minister very long. It seemed like I was meeting resistance every step of the way in the small rural church that had called me to serve. It was my first church, and I was certain that the leaders were against me. I resolved to prove my merit. I would be deep, theological, and aloof to their negativism. After all, I *had* been to Bible College. I would show those midwestern Septuagenarians that I had what it takes!

So I labored long and hard over my books. My sermons were punctuated profusely with words like *soteriology* and *pneumatology*. They collectively scratched their heads, and I wondered why I had not as yet gained their admiration and respect.

Furthermore, I resolved that my eight semester hours of Greek language study would not remain unused. I regaled the church with a variety of *tense, voice,* and *mood.* I honed my skills in *etymology* and *lexicography*. They did not respond.

I was about to give up the exposition of Greek as futile. But then, at a Wednesday Night Bible Study, a small breakthrough occurred. It was as if an angel of God had finally spoken and gotten through to the biggest blockhead of the bunch.

The lesson that evening was about love. It was a simple verse, really.

"This is the message you have heard from the beginning; We should love one another" (1 John 3:11, New International Version).

I knew that there was a wealth of information lurking under the surface. So I carefully exposited the word "love" while completely exasperating the people.

I correctly informed the group that there are three different Greek words for "love." I listed and explained *phileo, agape,* and *eros.* I had them look up scriptures that used *agape* and *phileo.* Then came the crucial moment of truth. Could they give me concrete applications of the three terms? So I asked them.

"Who would give me an example of one of these three kinds of love?"

Nobody answered. They just sat there and stared at me. It was one of those awkward moments I had come to expect.

"Who can give me an example of one of these kinds of love?" I asked again.

It was then that the breakthrough occurred. My own little daughter was raising her hand! My heart felt so proud. This little four and a half year old girl was about to put all of the people present to shame. She had been listening, and could give an example of *agape, phileo,* or *eros.*

"Sarah," I asked smugly. "Can you give us an example of one of these three types of love?"

She vigorously nodded. Confident.

"Sometimes," she blurted, "My Mommy takes a shower with my Daddy!"

I nearly died. My face went red. I glanced at my wife who had covered her face with her hands. And then it happened.

One of the Septuagenarians slapped his hand down on the table and let out a guffaw. He was laughing so hard that I doubt he even heard me confess that I had long since repented of showering with my wife.

But the others heard me, and their once shocked expressions were transformed into ones of unrestrained hilarity. Little Sarah, who had started it all, rocked back and forth in her chair and clapped her hands with glee!

I knew that I had lost them. The lesson was over! I did manage to gain enough composure to say a closing prayer, interrupted by an occasional, restrained snicker. Then I waited, shamefaced, for the group to leave.

They didn't leave, though. They stayed. They talked. They laughed some more. I couldn't believe it. I didn't understand it. My wife and daughter were the center of attention.

Then Mr. Septuagenarian walked over and put his arm around me. He laughed again, and said "I been tellin' everybody that you was human.

"They didn't believe me. Now that the truth is out, just relax. You don't have to impress us. Everybody here loves you. Just be yourself." He patted me on the back and went over to rib my wife some more.

That's when the angel voice got through to the biggest blockhead of the bunch. Me.

"Everybody here loves you, just be yourself."

My own little girl had probably given a better definition of the term "love" than even I could have imagined. And the weary congregation gave a wonderful application of the term.

Together, Sarah and that congregation had opened the door for a lifetime of loving, authentic ministry. I was so very relieved.

Converted, I swallowed my pride, walked over, and entered a lifetime of genuine ministry and laughter.

⌘ ⌘ ⌘

All Things Work Together For Good

Haven't we all experienced those "the car won't start and the payments won't quit" days of life? Sure we have! All of us know about those times when everything seems to go wrong, and the circumstances we face seem more than we can humanly bear.

The day after a heavy snowstorm, a little boy in the First Grade was found sleeping at his desk by his teacher.

"Jimmy, why in the world are you

sleeping at school? This isn't like you at all. I'm surprised at you!"

"It's them chickens," sleepy Jimmy answered. "It's all them chickens. It's them folks that are stealin' chickens again."

"What in the world do people stealing chickens have to do with your sleeping at school?" Jim's teacher demanded.

"Well, they've been stealin' our chickens for a long time now. Pa said next time they came round he was goin' to have a couple a' dead chicken thieves.

"Then, in that snowstorm last night, in the middle of the night, he heard them. Pa jumped up out of bed as fast as he could go, and grabbed his shotgun.

"He didn't take time to put on his trousers, just his boots. He ran out in his nightshirt. He loaded both barrels, and cocked them, too. He wasn't about to miss.

"Pa tip-toed through the snow 'til he got to the hen house. He had both fingers on those two triggers, and was easin' the door open real quiet with the barrel of the gun, when that ol' houn' dog of ours slipped up behind him an' run his cold wet nose up the back of Pa's nightshirt.

"And we was up all night pluckin' all those chickens!"

We know that there is nothing good about chicken thieves on a cold and snowy night. But a lot of fried chicken *is* a mighty good thing.

God has a way of taking our circumstances, no matter how painful, and bringing good out of them. He brings good out of our bad circumstances time after time.

The Apostle Paul, while imprisoned in Rome, wrote to the Philippian Church about his dire circumstances. He wrote:

"I want you to know that my circumstances have turned out for the greater progress of the gospel" (Philippians 1:12).

Later he would write to the Roman church "We know that God causes all things to work together for good to those who love God, to those who are called according to his purposes" (Romans 8:28).

Are you having one of "those days" again? Give your circumstances to God and claim His promises.

Then invite your neighbors over for all the fried chicken they care to eat.

⌘ ⌘ ⌘

Welcome Home

   My ninety year old Grandmother took a trip recently. It caused me to reminisce about the trips we used to take to her old house in the country.

She and Grandpa lived across two states from us. It was a long trip from the plains of Central Kansas to the rolling hill country of Eastern Oklahoma. Though the way was long, and we often traveled at night, we were never afraid. We were always excited. Our Dad knew the way, and no matter how stormy or dark it grew we knew we were safe.

In fact, it was more exciting to go home at night. Grandpa and Grandma lived on the prairie, and we could see the

> **"Inherit the Kingdom prepared for you. . ."**

soft light that glowed from their windows for miles as we came down out of the hills.

Inside, we knew that it would be warm and inviting. We knew that soon we would be wrapped up in the arms of people who really loved us.

In the distance she could see the brilliant light as it shone from the portals of the mansion that Christ had prepared for her.

Inside, she was welcomed by those she loves with shouts of celebration. Grandpa held out his arms to welcome her. Loved ones surrounded her and rejoiced with her in heaven's great love. And then Grandma asked for Jesus. He stepped forward, arms outstretched, and He welcomed her home.

"Come, ye blessed of My father, inherit the kingdom prepared for you from the foundation of the world" (Matthew 25:34)

⌘ ⌘ ⌘

Memories of Christmas Past

My wife and children probably think I have some wonderful memories of Christmas past; fond memories of trudging into the woods to cut a red cedar, and then taking it home to decorate with colored paper chains and popcorn strung on a string.

Frankly, that's not true, though I do prefer to cut my own tree. Yet cutting a tree is not a particular joy of mine. I cut my own tree because I am cheap (and my wife just said a hearty "Amen!").

My Christmas frugality has not been without problems. One year I brought home a nicely shaped, pasture grown beauty. It promptly proved to be a male tree by spreading its branches and pollinating everything in sight. It smelled like a whole family of frantic skunks had panicked and run rampant through our home. But that was a mild stink compared to the one my wife raised. ("Yes dear, you *did* tell me that you wanted to buy a tree this year. No, I *didn't* know there were male and female trees. Next year, I'll be more careful. O.K.?").

Another time I brought a lovely tree in, and it was exquisite when it was decorated. As it warmed itself in our cozy home, some tiny creatures who dwelt in the tree began to stir. Gnats. Thousands and millions of gnats began to wake and warm themselves in our home.

When we awoke the next morning our living room was one huge cloud of gnats! Of course, Mary was delirious with joy. Our children now have wonderful Yuletide memories of their fly-swatter swinging mother chasing their hysterically laughing father around and around a gnat filled room.

And now it's time to get a tree again. Every supermarket and corner store will have a good selection to choose from. Even the department stores will have a wide variety of artificial trees in an assortment of colors.

I am going to hold out for another hand cut red cedar.

Christmas isn't a tree. Christmas is the infant Son of God coming to proclaim the release of the captives, and the binding up of the wounds of the broken hearted.

Christmas is salvation, rich and full, freely offered by the son of God. Rich and full and free. Free. Free for the taking, just like my red cedar.

What price tag can you put on the true meaning of Christmas? God sent His only begotten Son.

Free!

Jesus gave His life for me. Free.

He died for me, by way of a tree.

Free.

⌘ ⌘ ⌘

Looking for Christmas

I didn't like Paul. I freely admit it. I just didn't, and when a Fourth grader makes up his mind, his mind is made up. Paul was, well, different. Odd.

"Probably a 'commie.'" That was my unspoken assessment, anyway, and I was up on those things. I'd heard all about it at Mike's Barber Shop.

"Them commies sneak in here masquerading as regular folks, and no one even suspects. Then one day, *POW!* The Big one!"

It wasn't too difficult for me, in those Cold War days, to imagine a communist spy infiltrating the ranks of Mrs. Lavender's Fourth Grade Class.

And it was obvious that Paul *was* a mastermind at brainwashing. He had Mrs. Lavender fooled, anyway. She fussed over him a lot. Especially at Christmas.

Paul didn't help us one bit around the classroom. He didn't decorate for the season, or string popcorn chains. He didn't glue one single colored paper ring in the chain that decorated the tree. He didn't rehearse carols in Music class for the school Christmas program, or participate in the drawing for the gift exchange.

Instead, every day, while we were getting ready for Christmas, Paul was going home early. It didn't make sense. Mrs. Lavender would wait for him by the door, pat him on the shoulder as he went out, and watch him walk down the hall.

"Yep. He's an atheist all right," I concluded.

December 23, 1964, just as our

Christmas party was about to begin, Paul marched to the cloak room, took his coat and his Howdy Doody lunch box, and went home early.

Nobody noticed, much, though. There were presents to unwrap and cookies to eat.

I jammed a rubber-tipped dart into the recently unwrapped blue plastic pistol I'd received, and thought about sticking it to the classroom window. No one would even notice in this Christmas chaos.

I pointed the gun at the window, but was startled to notice two eyes pressed against the glass and peeking in. It was Paul.

He hadn't seen me, and I delighted in the opportunity to shoot the "commie" right between the eyes.

Stealthily I crept across the festively decorated room. Snowflake cutouts danced on their strings as I drew a bead on Paul. He was just a few short inches away, and my finger tightened on the trigger.

"What's this?" I thought. I hesitated, surprised. Paul was crying. His cheeks were red from the cold and tears coursed down his face. I lowered the gun and stepped closer to the window. Paul turned and ran, and I watched him disappear out of sight.

The bus kids left class first, shouting "Merry Christmas!" I was the last one to speak to Mrs. Lavender at the door.

"Why doesn't Paul believe in God?" I asked.

Mrs. Lavender looked stunned.

"Oh, honey! Paul believes in God! Whatever gave you that idea?"

"He *didn't* help get ready for Christmas. He *didn't* sing the songs. He *didn't* stay for the party!" I just blurted it all out.

"Well . . ." her voice trailed off.

"And I saw him. Standing at the window. Watching us," I continued.

"Oh?" She glanced anxiously at the window, as though Paul might still be there.

"And he watched us for a long time."

"I see."

"And," I lowered my voice, "he was crying."

Mrs. Lavender placed her hand firmly on my shoulder.

"Paul and his family love God very

much. They are very good people."

"Then?"

"They are Jewish. They don't believe that Christ has been born yet. They are still looking for Him."

I didn't understand that, but I let it sink in. I felt tears well up in my own eyes.

"That's sad," I said. "How long will

> **"How long will they keep looking?"**

they keep looking?"

Mrs. Lavender shrugged and shook her head. She didn't know.

The she hugged me, just like I'd seen her hug Paul, and eased me into the hallway and closed her door.

I walked home through the cold, trying to comprehend Christmas without Jesus.

I couldn't do it.
I still can't.

⌘ ⌘ ⌘

Is There Room For Christ?
Luke 2:1-7

Christmas Eve travelers were crammed into the bus depot...pushing, shoving, swearing, complaining about the inevitable delays that accompany last

PAGE 132

minute holiday travel. Outside, the snow continued to fall. Beautifully and quietly it had come during the morning and by evening had enveloped everything in sight.

"Eat...eat...eat" flashed an inviting hot red neon message on the diner next door. A slushy brown path snaked its way to the small coffee shop. Inside, every table was occupied.

"There was no room in the inn," I mused while we waited impatiently for a table.

We had just been seated when a shabbily dressed man came in, carrying a baby wrapped in a dirty blue blanket. He was accompanied by a woman, shivering miserably. None of them were dressed for the cold.

They waited, warming themselves by the gas heater at the far end of the narrow room. We watched them while we drank hot coffee.

We noticed that the baby wore no coat, nor shoes. Her mother wore a threadbare brown corduroy coat, and her torn, wet canvas shoes testified to considerable time in the snow.

In silence they waited and warmed themselves. The harried waitress bussed a recently vacated table and nodded the pathetic trio towards it. The poor couple rewrapped the infant, clutched their coats to themselves, and walked back out into the cold.

A wave of sudden horror swept over me as I watched them go. I realized what I had allowed to happen.

A poor couple. A baby wrapped in swaddling clothes. No room. And now they were gone. Perhaps hungry. Maybe lonely. Definitely cold. And me? I had

Does Christ's Birth Make a Difference To You?

become the preoccupied inn keeper.

Does Christmas really make a difference? I like to think that it does, but that Christmas I had missed the message.

Don't miss the message! God's heart certainly has to ache over the human condition. We are the people whom He created to live in close harmony with Himself in peace and joy.

Instead, we are frail children of dust beset by evil and alienation. What could He do? What would He do?

He would send His Son. Surely the people He had created could learn to live and love from the Son of God.

But His birth would also bring the realization that some would find no room in their crowded lives for Jesus.

Is there any room in *your* life for Jesus? Whether His birth makes any difference in the world is left largely up to you.

⌘ ⌘ ⌘

"Got Your Wood Laid By?"

"Have you got your winter wood laid by?" That's a pretty relevant question considering these cold winter days we've experienced. I've been feeling a little sorry for our pioneer ancestors. During days like these it would be clearly evident whether or not they had prepared for hard times.

An unchinked crack in a log house would become a high velocity tunnel for the cold North wind. An unpatched roof would have resulted in their bed being blanketed with fine snow. An unattended fire would cause the drinking dipper to be firmly frozen in the water bucket by morning.

Another good indication of a family's

preparations would be the size of their woodpile. A wise family would be "future minded." Axes and cross-cut saws would be sharpened and ready at the first hint of frost.

Then daily, throughout the fall, the size of the woodpile would increase. It is no small wonder that the "winter wood" was the topic of many conversations.

"Got your wood laid by?" was a relevant question in the pre-chainsaw days.

I think it is still necessary to prepare for the future. Even more so in a spiritual sense. We aren't really certain what this New Year will hold for us. We may need plenty of spiritual "wood" laid by.

No year is completely "smooth skies and clear sailing." Common sense tells us that. Storms and heartaches may threaten, and we may need plenty of reserve spiritual supply. I hope that you are ready for the dark winter days of life.

My New Year's prayer is that God will ". . .supply all your needs according to His riches in glory in Christ Jesus" (Philippians 4:19).

⌘ ⌘ ⌘

A Great Teacher

"Yup, yup. Yup, yup." Uncle Charlie always answered in the affirmative, no matter what the question. If anyone ever had reason to voice negativism or complaint it was Uncle Charlie. Yet, he never did. His wide, impish grin characterized his positive attitude despite the many calamities life inflicted upon him.

When he was born sixty-plus years ago, the trauma of being a twelve pound infant too long in the birthing process diminished the supply of necessary oxygen to his brain. The midwife's forceps became a cruel instrument in the hands of fate that resulted in his jaw being broken.

But Charlie grew, and healed, and learned to play with toy trucks in the dirt like other boys. He learned to share, and to love, and to be obedient to his parents.

These were lessons that he would never forget. He entered school and made good progress. One day, however, while hitching up the team for his father, he was kicked in the head by a mule.

Time stood still for this little boy with a first grade education. He suffered irreparable brain damage.

He would never again attend school. He would never wear a graduation gown. Instead . . . he began a career as a teacher.

Uncle Charlie might be the greatest teacher I ever knew. You and I are "educated" people, and we've had some of the very best teachers at our disposal. These learned men and women may have taught us little in comparison with Charlie.

I've made study my lifetime vocation. I've studied Christology; Charlie taught

Christ-likeness. I study homiletics; Charlie taught happiness. I study ministry; Charlie taught the Master.

Uncle Charlie was an accomplished teacher, and never even knew it. He taught with his life.

All of us will miss him. He was a special person. It is possible that we never realized how special until now. All of the things that we hold dear in life are exemplified in the life of this patient gentle Brother and Uncle. It is never too late, though, to understand what his life taught.

Charlie taught us innocence. While his world tricked and cheated its way through war, conflict, and unrest, Charlie remained innocent. Oh, he was smart enough to lie or cheat if he wanted to. He just did not want to. He couldn't quote the Golden Rule, but he could sure live it. God smiles on the innocent.

"The way of the guilty is devious, but the conduct of the innocent is upright" (Proverbs 21:8). Charlie was innocent.

Charlie was as trusting as we ought to be. Every man was his friend. When his mother died, no one thought that he could live by himself. He surprised us all. Some people tried to take advantage of him, but his life teaches us the truth of Psalm 68:5:

"I will be a father to the fatherless, I will protect the widow."

Charlie taught us the importance of childlike faith and love.

"Allow the little children to come to me, and do not hinder them, for the kingdom of heaven belongs to such as these." (Mark 10:14-15). Jesus spoke those words.

I'm going to miss Charlie and what he represents. I will miss seeing him in blue bib-overalls and his gray striped engineer's cap, picking up aluminum cans along the road in front of his house.

I'm going to see him again, though. I'm certain of it. He will be wearing the graduation gown of glory as he intellectualizes with the living Christ.

This world labeled Uncle Charlie "retarded." Yet, he had more sense than many people in this world, and he proved it by his lifestyle.

Charlie would be pleased if we were to follow his example.

⌘ ⌘ ⌘

About the Author

Chuck Terrill lives in Augusta, Kansas, with Mary his wife of 24 years. They have three children; Chris, Ben, and Sarah, a daughter-in-law, Lisa, and a granddaughter, Ellana.

Chuck is a graduate of Ozark Christian College and Johnson Bible College and ministers with Haverhill Christian Church in rural Augusta, Kansas.

⌘ ⌘ ⌘

About the Illustrator

Bryan Clark, a 1976 graduate of Augusta High School, was born in El Dorado, Kansas, and has written and illustrated several books for his family, including:
Peanuts in the Blender, a book of ClarkFamily Stories (vol. 1), and **_Hawaii 3-Clarks in Paradise_**.

⌘ ⌘ ⌘